To Roy, for help and sympathy
when the computer goes wrong!
~ C F

To Mum, Dad, Rach, Tim, Ange
and the rest of the back-up!
~ L H

LITTLE TIGER PRESS
1 The Coda Centre, 189 Munster Road, London SW6 6AW
www.littletigerpress.com

First published in Great Britain 2005
This edition published 2008

Text copyright © Claire Freedman 2005 • Illustrations copyright © Louise Ho 2005
Claire Freedman and Louise Ho have asserted their rights to be identified as the
author and illustrator of this work under the Copyright, Designs and Patents Act, 1988

A CIP catalogue record for this book is available from the British Library

All rights reserved • ISBN 978-1-84506-825-7

Printed in China • LTP/1800/0451/0612

10 9 8 7 6 5 4 3 2 1

One Magical Morning

Claire Freedman

Louise Ho

LITTLE TIGER PRESS
London

In the shadowy woods,
one clear summer's morning,
Mummy took Little Bear
to see the day dawning.

The bears walked together
through grass drenched with dew.
Little Bear skipped,
as little bears do.

Little Bear gazed
as the sunrise unfurled.
"Up here," he cried,
"you can see the whole world!"

As the silvery moon
faded high in the sky,
Twinkle-eyed voles
came scurrying by.

And a little mouse gazed
as the morning sun
Melted the stars away,
one by one.

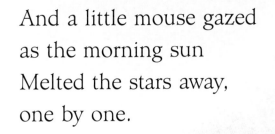

Fox cubs played while
the mist swirled like smoke,
Wrapping the trees
in its wispy cloak.

A pigeon coo-cooed
from a branch way up high.
Little Bear laughed,
"Look at me! Watch me fly!"

They stopped for a drink
at a babbling stream
And the sun turned the forest
soft pink, gold and green.

Bushy-tailed squirrels
scampered down trees,
Hunting for pine cones
hidden by leaves.

"Look, Mummy!" cried
Little Bear in delight.
As a mole burst, blinking,
into the light.

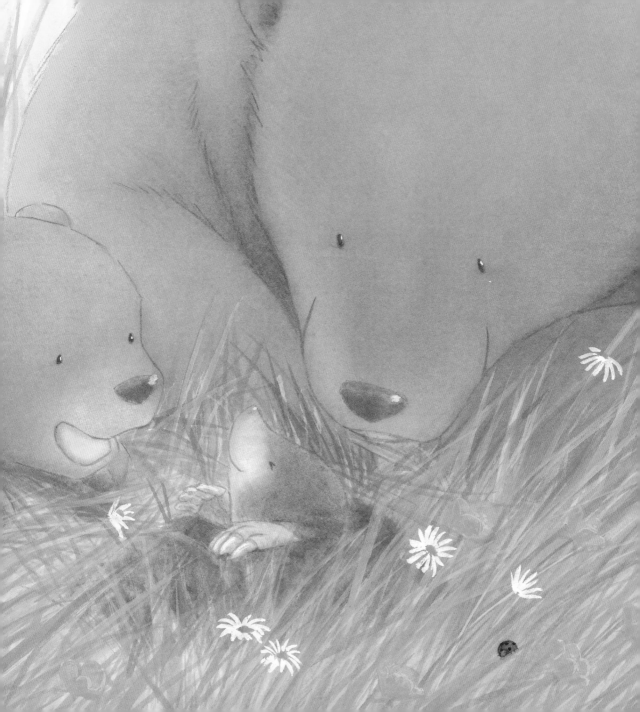

Mummy Bear smiled,
"Over here, take a peep!"
Bear's friend, Little Rabbit,
lay curled up asleep.

"Wake up, Little Rabbit,
come and play in the sun.
It's a beautiful day –
and it's just begun!"